PRESS Halifax, Nova Scotia, Canada

ISBN 0-929065-00-X
1989

For Steve, Amanda and Nicholas,
who never failed to take a poem
when it was passed.
J.B.

For Kelly and Ben.
K.R.K.

This book is meant to be an adventure, not only in the sharing of the poems with your child, but in the illustrations as well. If you look closely, you can discover many activities which grow out of the poems; activities you might want to try together.
I hope you enjoy these poems with your children as much as I have enjoyed sharing them with mine.

ISBN 0-929065-00-X
1989

Published by: Wildthings Press
3552 Windsor Street
Halifax, Nova Scotia
Canada B3K 5G8

Design: Kathy R. Kaulbach
Typesetting: Braemar Publishing Limited
Printing & Binding: Seaboard Printing,
Bedford, Nova Scotia

CANADIAN CATALOGUING
IN PUBLICATION DATA

Baskwill, Jane.

Pass the poems please
ISBN 0-929065-00-X

1. Children's poetry, Canadian (English) *
I. Kaulbach, Kathy R. (Kathy Rose), 1955–
II. Title

PS8553.A84P37 1989   jC811'.54   C89-098572-3
PZ8.3.B37Pa 1989

CONTENTS

OPEN A BOOK

Open a book
And you will find
People and places of every kind;
Open a book
And you can be
Anything that you want to be;
Open a book
And you can share
Wondrous worlds you find in there;
Open a book
And I will too,
You read to me
And I'll read to you.

COLLECTING

I found a shell and picked it up,
And all that day I had good luck,
Finding shells of every kind,
Collecting every shell I'd find.

I found a rock and picked it up,
And all that day I had good luck,
Finding rocks of every kind,
Collecting every rock I'd find.

I found a shoe and picked it up,
And all that day I had good luck,
Finding shoes of every kind,
Collecting every shoe I'd find.

Rocks and shells and all sorts of things
Like shoes or stamps or bits of string,
I like collecting things I find,
Collecting some of every kind.

MY PRIVATE COLLECTION

At dark, the stars,
So far away,
Twinkling in the night;
I've often wondered,
When they fall,
What happens to their light?
Do their lights
Go off
At once?
Or do they wait to see
If someone
Comes to
Pick them up—
Someone just like me.
And if I am
The lucky one,
Imagine what I'll see,
When I'm in bed,
Within my room,
A star that shines for me.

GETTING AROUND

Travel North,
Travel South,
Travel sea to sea;
Travel East,
Travel West,
To where you want to be;
Travel Here,
Travel There,
Travel far and wide;
By car,
By plane,
By camel train,
Hop on and take a ride.

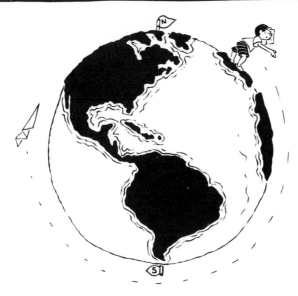

THE PAPER AIRPLANE

I made a paper airplane
I sailed it 'cross the floor,
It flew over my best friend's head
And then out through the door.
It headed north across the bridge
Then east through Lawrencetown,
It took a left at Doherty's
And hasn't yet been found.
I bet that plane is flying yet
I bet it's still around;
I'm gonna send it off again—
If it ever touches ground.

THE CLOSET

Quick, turn on the flashlight!
Shine it over here;
Did you hear that funny noise?
It came from over there;
Something brushed against my leg,
And tickled my left ear,
I think it's time we opened the door
And beat it out of here!

THE CAMPING SPOT

One day we set out camping,
Just my mom and me,
We went to find the perfect spot,
As perfect as can be;
We took our tent and sleeping bags,
A flashlight and my key,
We even took my teddy bear
To keep us company;
We finally found that perfect spot,
It really wasn't hard,
We knew the perfect camping spot
Was right in our back yard.

TREASURE HUNT MAP

WEATHER IS WEATHER

Whether it storms
Or whether it's fine
Weather is weather
Cloudy or fine.
Whether it rains
Or whether it snows
Weather is weather
However it goes.

IT'S RAINING AGAIN

It's raining again and I'm mad,
It's ruined the plans that I had,
I wanted to play
Outdoors today
But it's raining again and I'm mad.

It's raining again and I'm glad,
I've new rubber boots from my dad,
A rain hat that's blue
And a macintosh, too,
So it's raining again and I'm glad.

MUD MARCH

It's hard to keep the beat
With this mud on my feet,
As it oozes and it goozes,
And it squishes and it squoozes,
As it tries to suck my boooots off
When I'm marching in the mud.

FAVOURITE FIT

Don't throw away my sweatshirt!
I still wear those jeans;
I know they have some holes,
Especially near the knees;
That's my very best sock!
I know it's not a pair;
I'm saving it inside my drawer
By last year's underwear!
You're throwing away my favourites,
I don't like it one small bit,
If you throw away my favourites
I'll only have things that fit!

GROWING UP

I've learned to ride my bicycle,
I've learned to tie my shoe,
I've even pulled my loose tooth out,
And my sister's, too;
I've learned to say my ABC's,
And to count to ten;
I've even learned to dial the phone
So I could call my friend;
I've grown taller than my sister,
And my best friend, too,
All my pant legs are too short,
And my shirt sleeves, too!
My mother says I'm growing,
She says I'm doing fine;
But I'm worried I'll be all grown up
By the time that I reach nine!

HAS ANYBODY SEEN MY THINGS?

Has anybody seen my sock?
Or what about my shoe?
Has anybody seen my hat?
The one that's just brand new?
Has anybody seen my book?
Or what about my bear?
I have a place for all my things—
I just can't remember where!

IN GRANDMA'S ATTIC

Up in Grandma's attic
I found a great old trunk;
She says there's not much in it,
She says it's full of junk;
But I know what Grandma doesn't,
It's full of magic things;
Like hero's hats, and kingly jewels,
And drapes for fairy's wings;
I think I'll keep it secret,
Between just you and me,
When we dress up together,
Just think what we can be!

THAT'S NATURAL

Stars come out at night,
Lightning bugs flash bright,
Eagles soar in flight,
That's natural.

Sea shells wash ashore,
One seed leads to more,
An apple leaves a core,
That's natural.

Water's ice when cold,
Our earth is very old,
A bat's wing can fold,
That's natural.

The world is full of marvels,
They're just waiting to be found;
Taking time to notice
Every sight, smell, touch, taste, sound...
That's natural.

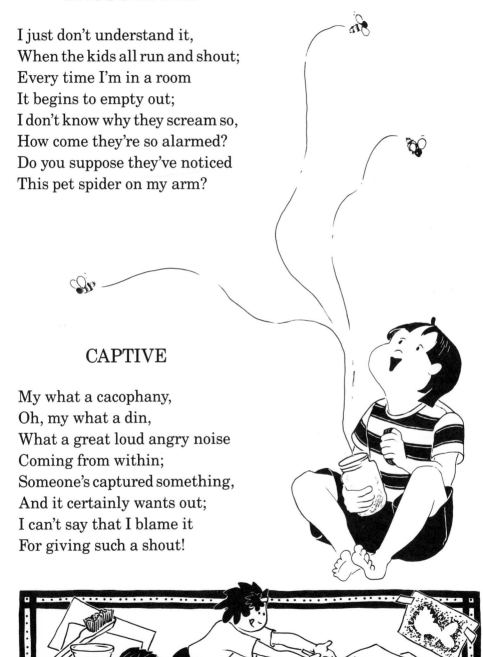

UNUSUAL PET

I just don't understand it,
When the kids all run and shout;
Every time I'm in a room
It begins to empty out;
I don't know why they scream so,
How come they're so alarmed?
Do you suppose they've noticed
This pet spider on my arm?

CAPTIVE

My what a cacophany,
Oh, my what a din,
What a great loud angry noise
Coming from within;
Someone's captured something,
And it certainly wants out;
I can't say that I blame it
For giving such a shout!

19

HOW MANY DAYS IN A WEEK?

Just how many days are in a week?
I never get them straight;
No matter how I count them
I end up counting eight.
The trouble with the days, you see,
Is they're always going by;
I never know just when to stop
No matter how I try.

TIME OUT

It's time to go to Brownies,
It's time to go to school,
It's time to go to piano lessons
Or the swimming pool;
It's always time for something,
Sometimes it's time for bed,
Some day I'd like to not have time
And stay at home instead!

20

TICK TICK TOCK

Tick, tick, tock,
Listen to the clock;
Strike one,
Strike two,
Strike the hour when it's new,
Tick, tick, tock.

WHAT'S INSIDE?

What's in your pocket, your pocket, your pocket,
What's in your pocket, your pocket today?

I've a wriggly worm that can squiggle and squirm,
And a handful of sand and a blue rubberband;
That's what I have in my pocket, my pocket,
That's what I have in my pocket today.

What's in your bucket, your bucket, your bucket,
What's in your bucket, your bucket today?

I've some brushes and soap and a coil of old rope,
And a few bottle caps and some worn-out old snaps,
That's what I have in my bucket, my bucket,
That's what I have in my bucket today.

What's in your small hand, your small hand, your small hand,
What's in your small hand, your small hand today?

I've the hand of a friend with whom I will spend
A very nice day as together we play,
That's what I have in my small hand, my small hand,
That's what I have in my small hand today.

THE EGGS

I wonder how they change in there;
I wonder how they grow;
I wonder how it looks inside;
I wonder when I'll know
Just what's going on in there;
Just what has come about;
The only way I'm sure I'll know
Is to wait 'til they hatch out.

FEELY
BOX

HIDING PLACES

I've hidden beneath the table,
I've hidden behind the door,
I've hidden inside a laundry bag,
And under a rug on the floor;
I've hidden in zillions of places,
And I just don't understand,
How come Samuel finds me
No matter where I am?

THE GREAT DETECTIVE

Sh-h-h-h-h, the Great Detective
Is out to solve a case;
I want to dust this room for prints,
I know this is the place;
Sh-h-h-h-h, don't interrupt me,
I'll have this solved real soon—
Aw, Mom, how could you find your keys?
I've looked for them since noon!

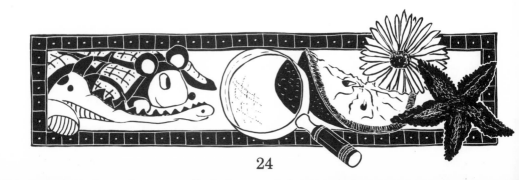

HIDDEN

In my house there is a room,
And in my room there is a bed,
And tucked in bed,
You can't see where,
Is a tiny, little teddy bear.

LISTEN TO THE WIND

Listen to the wind speak,
Listen to her roar,
Listen to her grumble
As she slams the kitchen door;
Then listen to her whisper
Something soft and low;
Listen and the wind will tell you
Everything she knows.

THE ESCAPE

Hey, there goes my favourite scarf!
And look, there goes my hat!
That looks just like my brand new blouse!
What should I make of that?
Ooops, there goes my poster,
And my lucky deck of cards;
It seems the wind's been busy,
Now my room is in the yard!

BLOW WIND

North wind
Wild wind
Cold wind
Blow;
Storm wind
Roar wind
Blow wind
Snow.
South wind
Calm wind
Warm wind
Bring;
Rain wind
Splash wind
Blow wind
Spring.

MY TOWN

I live in a little town,
It really is quite small,
It only has one corner store,
A Co-Op and that's all,
It doesn't have a traffic light,
It doesn't have a bus,
But it has grass and shady trees
And lots of room for us.

MY FRIENDS

Courtney lives next door to me,
Caleb, two doors down,
Jeremy lives far away
On the other side of town;
Would you like to meet them?
I'll call them on the phone;
Then we can plan to stop for tea
Some day when they're at home.

MY FAVOURITE PLACE

When walking down the sidewalk
I jump over all the cracks,
And when I get to Fifth and Main
I cross the railroad tracks,
I turn left at Mrs. Bailey's,
Then right at the candy shop,
And then I'm at my Grandpa's house,
My favourite place to stop.

PACKING

I have to pack my things, my things,
I have to pack my things;
I can't decide just what to take
But I have to pack my things.
Shall I take my—
Teddy bear, my bike, my raft, my ball?
My dog, my car, my rubber boots,
The coat I got last fall?
My ball of string, my book, my comb,
My flashlight or my snake?
I have to pack my things, my things,
But I don't know what to take.

LEAVING

It looks like we are moving
And I'm really, really sad,
I have to leave my favourite tree
And the secret fort I had,
I have to leave my ant hill
And the flock of birds I feed,
Who will water the marigolds
I planted from a seed?
Dad said someone's moving in,
I sure hope they're smart,
So they can read the notes I left
Which tell them where to start.

PASS THE POEMS PLEASE

Pass the poems please,
Pile them on my plate;
Put them right in front of me
For I can hardly wait
To taste each tangy word,
To try each tasty rhyme,
And when I've tried them once or twice
I'll try them one more time;
So, pass the poems please,
They just won't leave my head,
I have to have more poems
Before I go to bed.